TURKISH DELIGHT

BENJAMIN GROOM

Turkish Delight

Past Venus Press
London 2005

Past Venus Press

is an imprint of

THE *Erotic* Print Society

EPS, 1st Floor, 17 Harwood Road,
LONDON SW6 4QP

Tel (UK only): 0871 7110 134
Email: eros@eroticprints.org
Web: www.eroticprints.org

© 2005 MacHo Ltd, London UK

ISBN : 1-904989-06-3

Printed and bound in Spain by BookPrint S.L., Barcelona

first to avoid the chance of being caught here with one of the guests, which was strictly against the rules, but he couldn't very well say no. She had certainly changed, he reflected. Now she acted as though she wanted nothing more than to have sex with him. He smiled as he mixed the potent cocktail for the two of them. Obviously he had made an indelible impression upon her before Onan had managed to spirit her away. He was flattered. He had conveniently forgotten that Lucy had been semi-comatose when he had so nearly succeeded in fucking her, but he could still see his large shiny cockhead about to push its way through the blonde hair of her cunt, only to be cruelly interrupted by the arrival of Madame Cari; it was an extraordinary reversal of fortune, he mused to himself; as he led the way, drinks in hand, through to the small sun lounge that ran, like an enclosed veranda, behind the office. Softly glowing lamps gave an intimate feel to the room and there were palms and plants in brass pots, cheerful, gaudy wall hangings and large exotic cushions with little sewn-in mirrors strewn over low divans. The effect was pleasant enough, thought Lucy, as they placed their drinks on a low table next to one of the divans.

"My," said Lucy after they'd sat down, "I do believe this drink is going to my head!

Would you be so kind as to get me my cigarettes? They're over there, behind you, on top of my handbag."

Hasad turned to get the cigarette packet; when he looked back at her, he noticed that Lucy had shifted her position so that her skirt rose up over her thighs giving him a tempting glimpse of her white cotton panties. She's done that on purpose, he thought. It's surely a signal that she's available... for sex!

"Do you get lonely here, Hasad, or do you have a girlfriend to keep you company?"

The big, ugly man grinned, his eyes glued to her provocative display of her pussy covered only by a layer of thin material. He took a big gulp of his cocktail.

"No girlfriend, Madame. Only me."

"Do you like to fuck girls, Hasad? Or do you prefer boys?" she asked teasingly.

Hasad stopped grinning.

"I would like to fuck you, Madame Lucy," he husked. "I would like to fuck you very much..."

Now Lucy smiled and leaned over towards him, her delicate fingers quickly finding the zipper of his pants. In a second she had fished out his rock hard penis and started to masturbate him gently, so that the foreskin skimmed back and forth over the shining rosy glans of his cock. Bending down, she took the monster into her warm, wet mouth. She was relieved to find that his personal hygiene was of an entirely acceptable standard.

Hasad was taken aback at this girl's extraordinary self-confidence; he found it provocative and exciting that she appeared to be taking the initiative in this way, but he also felt that for once he was on unfamiliar ground and that control of the situation was slipping away from him. So be it, he thought. As long as I get to fuck her tight little cunt, and maybe her even tighter little asshole, I don't really care. She'll soon find out who is boss. But in the meantime, I'll just let her suck my cock. It's so relaxing... so very... relaxing.

A few minutes later, Lucy stood and looked down at the gently snoring night manager, his large, half-erect cock still shiny with her saliva. A smirk of triumph played around her lips. So easy! she thought. Slipping that powder in his drink was like taking candy from a kid. He'll wake up with nothing but a slight hangover tomorrow, and if one of the guests wakes him up he'll have some explaining to do – with his cock hanging out of his pants! She made her way to the waiting taxi.

* * *

Following Onan's directions, John had no difficulty finding the tiny room with the peephole. He just couldn't resist taking a quick look at the unsuspecting English girl before announcing his presence. He lifted the guard and put his eye to the tiny opening, gasping from the sight that met his gaze. Onan hadn't mentioned that she was a redhead. And she very definitely was, he mused, taking in the bright triangle of flame-coloured pubic curls at the "vee" of her beautifully moulded thighs. She was busily drying herself off after her bath, and as she bent and twisted to reach all the remote parts of her innocent young body, John had a good preview of all the luscious charms he would soon sample for the first time.

Finally she hung up the towel and surveyed herself in the full-length mirror mounted on the back of the bathroom door. Her full rounded breasts jutted proudly out in front of her, their rosy tips slightly erect from the rubdown she had given herself.

It was obvious she had only recently discovered the attractiveness of her own body and was on the verge of enjoying it with a man for the first time. She ran her hands appreciatively over the soft resilience of her breasts and down over the flat plane of her white belly, slipping them over the gentle slope of her flaring hips to trail on down to the half-moon buttocks behind. She smiled at her image, practicing an alluring sensual look that she no doubt expected to use on her waited lover.

John chuckled softly to himself. Little did she know, he thought, patting the forged note in his pocket, that her boyfriend wouldn't be the one to run his hands over that virginal young body and enter her tight, unused little virgin cunt. Not if everything goes according to plan, he added to himself. He waited until she had slipped on a hip-length sheer nightgown that did little to hide her delicious curves from his view, and then he left the secret observation room.

"W-who is it?" her hesitant voice fluted from inside the door when he had knocked softly. Her voice was a mixture of fear and anticipation, John sensed as he listened to her opening and closing what must be a closet inside. Probably she hadn't really adjusted herself to the idea of losing her virginity, even to a man she loved, and undoubtedly every time she thought the moment was nearer she became filled with anxiety.

"A friend of Henry," he told her in a low voice through the door. Henry was the man she had been waiting for, and Onan had been sure there would be no trouble in approaching the girl if she thought John was delivering a message from him. There was a sudden flurry of movement inside, and John smiled to himself – Onan had been right. Then the door swung open, and he saw that she had put on a long robe over her short nightgown.

"I was expecting Hasad, the night clerk," the girl said breathlessly. "Come in. Where *is* Henry?" she intoned anxiously looking over John's shoulder. "And how do I know you're a friend of his?" she suddenly asked, suspicion flitting over her face.

"My name is John Dean," he told her in a soothing voice, his eyes crinkling sympathetically as he smiled at her. "And I have a note for you from Henry." He handed her the envelope containing the expertly forged message and waited for her to open it.

The girl looked at the thin blue paper in her fingers as though it were a snake that might bite her, and then hastily ripped it open, her eyes passing quickly over John's face as if trying to read what was in the note from his expression.

He watched her eyes flick back and forth over the words, unhappy disbelief clouding her face; then she read it again more slowly, forming the sounds on her lips as though it were written in a foreign language. Her hands began to tremble uncontrollably as she read and reread the message, and her full sensual lips slowly parted and turned downward as she began to cry.

"I-I don't believe it," she sobbed. "It's not possible." She turned her deep green eyes up to meet John's gaze, her lips quivering like little wet fruits. Tears were welling up in her eyes as she looked up at him helplessly.

"Did you see what he wrote?" she cried in a broken voice, holding the note out for him to read. Henry loves me – it can't be true what this says!"

Dear Charlotte,

I simply couldn't bear to tell you this in person, therefore, John is bringing this to you. I've decided that it would not be fair if I took advantage of your youthful innocence. I could never forgive myself afterwards. Vicky Greenbaum and I have been in love for a long time, and as soon as she can get a divorce from her husband, we will be married.

I know you will never forgive me, but this way I can at least live with my conscience.

Sincerely, and with all my heart, Henry

P.S. John has kindly consented to see that you are safely returned to Istanbul.

"I'm so sorry," John spoke gently to her. She was standing before him with tears now streaming down her cheeks, her exquisitely pretty face contorted by her grief. Pretending anger, he wadded the paper in his fingers and flung it moodily at the wall. "Why did I have to be the one?" he shouted. "Why did I have to meet you this way?"

The young Charlotte glanced up at him

through her tears and a sob caught in her throat – then without warning she fell into his automatically opening arms and pressed her face into his chest.

Her whole body was shaking with the force of her crying, and John wrapped his arms around her, cooing softly into her ear. He could feel the fullness of her firmly ripe breasts jostling against him through the material of their clothing, and he fought to keep from grinding his awakening loins up into her shuddering belly below. All in good time, he told himself, all in good time, as he continued comforting the young girl huddled in his arms.

Gradually she seemed to calm down, the silences between her body-wracking sobs getting longer and longer, and finally she shifted and removed herself from his encircling arms, running to the bathroom to repair the damage the tears had done to her face.

After a long time, she emerged again, attempting a brave smile. "I'm being very foolish," she said as though she had spent years instead of minutes recovering from the shock of the note. "It's something that everybody goes through, and I can manage it too. It's the first time that hurts," she added, trying to act older than her years, but then she suddenly broke down again and without hesitation hurried to nestle once more in John's arms.

She calmed down more quickly this time, and John led her to a chair and made her sit down.

"What you need is a cigarette," he told her soothingly. He held the packet out and she shakily took one gratefully taking a deep drag of the warm smoke into her lungs as John lit it for her. Onan knew that the girl smoked, and he had had this package made especially for her. The tobacco was drenched in the strong resin from the upper leaves of the marijuana plant, and it wouldn't take many lungfuls for her to begin feeling the effect of the conscience-killing drug.

John lit one for himself and continued to listen attentively, showing understanding mingled with a flirting interest. Almost at once she had begun to relax from the effects of the soothing smoke, and in a few minutes she was smiling warmly, running her eyes approvingly over his ruggedly handsome features.

At least Henry had the decency to send someone interesting, she thought to herself. She was wondering how long she would have to wait to kiss John's sensual lips without seeming too callous. But who cares about appearances anyway, she reflected bitterly as she finished the drug-ridden cigarette and stubbed it out in the ashtray.

She stood up slowly, and with a toss of her head that sent her flaming red hair flying back over her shoulders, she took John's hand and pulled him up from the chair where he was watching her with amused, wide-open eyes. She recognized the lust in them from her recent near-affair with Henry, and she liked being looked at that way.

John rose slowly from his seat, and, smiling greedily down at her upturned face, pressed his slightly parted lips wetly over hers.

Jesus, he was thinking as her tongue answered his spearing probe up between her open lips. Every day is like Christmas! He had never before found it so easy to get his way with women. It's all in who you know, he chuckled to himself. John felt her arms slipping up around his neck to pull him down tighter onto her hungry mouth; he let his fingers glide unobtrusively down to explore the inviting valley of where her buttocks joined. There was no resistance to this intimate caress, just an almost imperceptible shift in her balance, one that favoured an easier access to her bottom's divide, and he knew it was going to be all right.

"I think you'd better drive back to Istanbul with me, Charlotte, there's no reason for you to stay out here. My... sister is waiting in the taxi. You can stay with us tonight and we'll put you in touch with the right people tomorrow. Here, let me get your suitcase... I'll help you pack."

Just a few of our many titles for sale...

Lazonby's Heiress
Little does Alison realise her duties as secretary of Lazonby Hall include being a sexual 'play-doll' for the lascivious desires of all in the house. Mrs. Simpson is Mistress of the Hall in name, but now it's Alison's luscious young body that holds the title!
£7.50

Helen's Southern Comfort
In the heat of the night Danny watches as his innocent wife is treated to pleasures she has never experienced before by his well-endowed neighbour. So begins a journey of sexual discovery for the Nielson's that takes them to the very edges of extreme sexual practices.
£7.50

Highland Seduction
Amanda's visit to the Scottish Highlands becomes a nightmare as increasingly bizarre sexual ordeals are heaped upon her by the predatory residents of Sandaid Manor. Even her handsome husband cannot save her from the degrading ordeal to which she is subjected.
£7.50

The Education of Catherine Peterson
Bored, beautiful Catherine wants a job with her husband's firm. She gets one only to discover her husband's infidelity. Soon, the couple are sucked into a vortex of lust from which they cannot escape – even if they wanted to. Office sexual politics were never quite like this.
£7.50

Los Angeles Girl & Punishment for Claudia
Special double edition. Model and virgin, Della, finds herself giving more than she wants to on her photo-shoots in Los Angeles Girl. Claudia is a Nazi spy in wartime USA with a penchant for spanking, being spanked and submissive sex in Punishment for Claudia.
£12.50

The End